When Brucie Came To Play

When Brucie Came To Play

AND OTHER STORIES

by Esther Bailey

BEACON PRESS : BOSTON

Contents

1. When Brucie Came To Play

ONE day Brucie came to Alan's house to play all day.

He played with Alan's trucks.

He played with Alan's football and his blocks. Sometimes Alan let Brucie ride his racing car.

Alan had fun when Brucie came to play.

Brucie thought of things to do that Alan wouldn't have thought of doing by himself. And Alan thought of things to do that Brucie wouldn't have thought of doing.

They threw Alan's football to each other across the yard. They slid down the slippery grass on the hill beside Alan's house. They ran up the stairs in Alan's house and then bumped all the way down on their bottoms.

Alan liked Bruce. Bruce liked Alan. They were friends.

But sometimes Alan wished Brucie were not there. He wished Brucie would go home to stay with his own mother.

When Alan and Brucie wanted to play with the same dump truck, Alan's mother said they could play with different trucks. When Brucie wanted to ride Alan's racing car, Alan's mother said they had to take turns.

Once Brucie fell and bumped his head. It hurt so much he cried. Alan's mother picked Brucie up and held him on her lap until he felt better. Alan felt like sitting on his mother's lap too, but he couldn't because Brucie was there.

He wished Brucie would go home.

But later, when it was time for Brucie to go home to his own house and his own mother, Alan didn't want him to go.

After Brucie had gone, Alan went outside to play. He played with all his trucks all by himself. He rode his racing car up and down the driveway. He didn't have to take turns with anybody.

He slid down the slippery grass on the hill beside his house. It was still fun, but he wished Brucie were sliding with him. He found his football in the yard and threw it up in the air. He caught it, then threw it up again. If Brucie had been there, he could have thrown it to Brucie, and Brucie could have thrown it back to him.

Alan went inside. His mother was sitting in a chair reading. Alan climbed up into her lap. He talked to her, and she listened to him, just to him. Mother read Alan a story. She read it to him, just to him.

2. The Steep Hill

JEFF stood in front of his house eating his toast. Grandmother always spread on lots of jam. Some of the jam slid down onto Jeff's hand. He licked it off and wiped his hand on his shirt.

Jeff walked to the curb to see if any cars were coming.

"Get back on the sidewalk!" Grandmother called from the front door.

Jeff looked down. He was standing in the street. How had that happened? He thought he was standing on the curb. He jumped backwards onto the sidewalk. He felt like trying it again, but Grandmother was still standing at the door.

"Stay on the sidewalk!" Grandmother called again.

Jeff walked to the house next door to play with Stevie. But Stevie wasn't home. Jeff walked to the end of the block to see if Sandra could play with him. Sandra wasn't home either.

4

Jeff turned the corner and looked down the hill. Maybe he could find someone to play with at the bottom of the hill.

He started down. It was steep. He had never walked down this hill alone before. It looked even steeper on the other side of the street. There were no cars going up the hill. There were none going down. He crossed the street and ran all the way to the bottom.

He ran around the corner.

"Beep beep!" a voice said.

Jeff almost bumped into a boy riding his tricycle.

"This is my motorcycle," the boy said. "I have to go fast. Beep beep!"

Jeff stepped out of the motorcycle's way and watched. He liked the noise the boy was making. It sounded like a motorcycle going fast.

Jeff made the noise too.

"You can't do that," the boy said. "You aren't riding anything."

Jeff kept on making the noise.

"You can ride my sister's tricycle," the boy said. "She is Susan, and she's taking a nap. I'm Timmy. I'm too old to take naps."

Timmy ran to his garage and came out with a tricycle. It was a small tricycle, but Jeff could still ride it.

Jeff and Timmy raced up and down the sidewalk. They made loud noises when they went fast, and soft noises when they slowed down.

"Timmy!" a voice called.

5

"Is that your grandmother?" Jeff asked.

"No, it's my mother," Timmy said, and he raced to the other end of the sidewalk. Jeff followed him.

"Timmy, come here!"

"Your mother sounds cross," Jeff said.

Timmy turned around and raced back to his mother. Jeff stayed where he was.

Jeff watched Timmy's mother scold Timmy. He watched her send Timmy into his house. Jeff watched Timmy's mother walk toward him, and he jumped off Susan's tricycle. She looked very cross.

But Timmy's mother didn't scold Jeff. She didn't even look at him. She leaned over to pick up Susan's tricycle, then hurried back into her yard.

Suddenly Jeff felt very far from home.

He ran around the corner and up the steep side of the hill. He crossed the street and ran to the top of the hill. Jeff turned the corner. He saw his street. He saw his house.

Grandmother was at the front door looking for him. Jeff ran and threw his arms around her legs.

6

3. *You Are Stupid*

ANNE put her dress on by herself one morning.

Mother was pleased.

Father thought she looked very nice.

Her brothers only laughed.

"You put it on back to front," George said.

"You are stupid," Brian said.

Anne began to feel cross. "I did it on purpose so I could reach the buttons by myself," she said.

Anne felt so cross she spilled her juice all over the breakfast table.

Father frowned.

George laughed.

"You are stupid," Brian said again.

That made Anne so cross she felt like crying.

After breakfast Anne started to put on her shoes. They were buckle shoes, and Anne could fasten them by herself.

Something snapped. A shoe strap came off in her

hand. Anne sat down on the floor and cried. She cried even harder when Mother took her shoes off and put on the sneakers with holes in the toes.

Then it was time for Father to go to work, for George and Brian to go to their school, and for Anne to go to her school.

Anne frowned all the way to nursery school. She didn't like her sneakers. But she forgot about them when she reached her school. She ran to the door ahead of her mother. She wanted to tell Mrs. Perkins that she had dressed herself.

But the lady who stood at the door wasn't Mrs. Perkins. She didn't even look like Mrs. Perkins.

"Where is my teacher?" Anne asked.

"Mrs. Perkins couldn't be here today," the lady answered. "I'm going to be your teacher this morning. My name is Mrs. Jones." She walked with Anne into the classroom.

Anne didn't think she liked Mrs. Jones. She started to go back to her mother so that her mother could take her home again, but when she saw Janet and Michael playing in the sandbox, she changed her mind.

Anne watched Janet and Michael making sand pies.

They didn't pay any attention to her. Anne grabbed the sieve Janet was using.

"I need this," Anne said. She moved to the other end of the sandbox.

Janet cried.

"Give Janet her sieve!" Michael shouted.

8

Anne didn't want the sieve anymore. She threw it across the sandbox to Janet. "You are stupid!" Anne shouted.

Mrs. Jones came up to Anne. "Would you like to paint?" she asked.

"No."

Anne sat down on a chair by herself. She watched Mrs. Jones help some of the children get into their smocks. She watched the children take paintbrushes with long shiny handles and fat bristles from a jar. They began to paint.

Suddenly Anne was tired of just sitting. She bent over and tore all the rubber off the front of her sneakers; then she got up and walked over to one of the easels.

Michael was making a bright yellow ball in the middle of his paper. Some of the paint ran down and splashed onto the floor.

9

"You made a mess," Anne said. She walked to an easel that wasn't being used. "I want to paint!" Anne shouted.

Mrs. Jones gave her a brush and three jars of paint. Anne dipped her brush into each jar. She painted a thick line across her paper. Then she poured all the colors into one jar and mixed them together. The paint was thick and gooey. She spread it all over her paper. It looked like a gray mud puddle.

Anne tore her painting from the easel and threw it onto the floor. "I need more paper!" she screamed.

Mrs. Jones pinned a clean sheet of paper onto the easel. She gave Anne fresh jars of paint. Then she helped Anne clean her brush.

Ann dipped her clean brush into the blue paint jar. She made some thick blue lines. She liked the bright color.

Mrs. Jones liked it too. She told Anne that blue was her favorite color.

Anne told Mrs. Jones that she had dressed herself that morning. Then she told her why she was wearing sneakers instead of her buckle shoes.

4. *Alan's Hats*

ALAN had three important hats—a fireman's hat, a cowboy hat, and a baseball hat. He hung them on a low hook inside the closet door. He could reach any hat he wanted to wear.

If Alan was wearing his cowboy hat and a fire engine clanged down the street, he put on his fireman's hat. That helped him feel like a fireman.

Sometimes Alan's tricycle seemed like a horse, so he put on his cowboy hat. Then he was a cowboy.

The hat Alan wore most often was his baseball hat. He wore it when he played ball. He wore it when he went places. He wore it to the store with his mother. He wore it visiting friends with his mother and father and sister, or to church. It was a nice hat. If Alan pulled it down over his eyes, people couldn't see his face unless he wanted them to.

One day Alan wanted to wear his cowboy hat. He opened the closet. His fireman's hat was on one hook.

His baseball hat was on the next. The third hook was empty.

"Mother!" he shouted.

"What?" Mother called from the basement, where she was doing the laundry.

"I need my cowboy hat!" Alan shouted.

"Look in the closet."

"It isn't there." Alan stomped down the basement stairs. "You have to find my cowboy hat!" he said.

"Did you look in the closet?" Mother asked.

"Yes."

"Why don't you wear your fireman's hat?" Mother asked.

"I have to wear my cowboy hat." Alan stood on tip-toe to watch the clothes slosh around in the washing machine. Then he went outside to ride his tricycle.

Alan remembered something and ran inside again.

"You have to find my cowboy hat!" he screamed.

"It's time for lunch," Mother said.

"First I have to have my cowboy hat." Alan began to feel cross with his mother.

"Let's think about where it could be while we eat," Mother said. She put Alan's soup on the table. Alan ate one mouthful. "Let's think now," he said.

"All right," Mother said. "Where were you the last time you wore your cowboy hat?"

"I don't know."

"Were you in the garage?"

"No."

"Maybe you were in your room," Mother said.

"Maybe I was in the attic."

"Maybe you were," Mother said.

"Or maybe I was in the basement," Alan said. "Maybe you washed it in the washing machine." He giggled.

"Could you have put it in your toy box? Or left it in the yard under the swing?" Mother asked.

Alan looked in his toy box in the kitchen. There weren't any hats in there. He looked out of the kitchen window. He couldn't see any hats under the swing. Alan sat down again and finished his soup.

"Let's think some more," Alan said.

Mother thought hard. "The last time I saw you wearing your cowboy hat, you were playing on the stairs," she said.

Alan thought hard. "The last time I felt me wearing

my cowboy hat I was——" Alan ran upstairs to his room. He crawled under his bed. He crawled out again with something wide and dusty. He ran back to his mother.

"You don't have to find it for me," Alan shouted. "I thought about where it was all by myself!" He was wearing his cowboy hat.

5. *Nobody Knows I'm Here but Me*

"ANNE, for the last time, get out!" Anne's brother George slammed his bedroom door in Anne's face.

It was raining. It had been raining all morning, and Anne didn't have anything to do. She didn't have anyone to play with. She couldn't find any place where she wanted to play.

George and Brian didn't want Anne to play in their room with them.

Father was in the living room working at his desk. He didn't want anyone to talk to him.

Mother was in the kitchen cleaning drawers and shelves. She didn't mind Anne talking, but she was too busy to listen to what Anne had to say.

Anne decided to go back into the kitchen anyway. Mother was cleaning the spice shelf. Anne took the covers off some of the jars so that she could smell what was inside.

"Why don't you play in your room?" Mother asked

while she was putting the spice jars away.

"I played there," Anne said.

Mother got down on her hands and knees to take the pots and pans out of a drawer. They made such a clatter she wouldn't hear what Anne was saying if she wanted to say anything.

Anne walked upstairs to her room. Her dolls, her dolls' clothes, and her dollhouse furniture were scattered all over the floor and the bed. Anne didn't feel like playing in there. She picked up her favorite doll and walked out into the hall.

George and Brian were talking and laughing together in their bedroom. Mother was still clattering around in the kitchen. Father was being quiet in the living room, and the rain was still splashing against the window in the hall.

Anne went over to the attic door and opened it. The stairs were dark and scary, but if she stood on the second stair, she could reach the light switch. She snapped it, and the light over the landing halfway up came on.

16

Anne ran back to her room. She carried her doll's cradle to the landing. She put her doll in the cradle, then went back to her room for her own blanket.

Anne sat on her blanket on the landing and held her doll. The rain pattered down onto the attic roof above her head. Even with the door open, the sounds from the rest of the house were very far away.

"This is my place," Anne whispered to her doll. "I know where everybody else in the house is, but nobody knows I'm here but me."

6. When Will Grandmother Come Back?

JEFF sat up in bed. It was still dark.

"Is it time to get up?" Jeff asked.

Mother came to his bed.

"No, it's too early," she said. "Lie down and go back to sleep." She tucked the covers in around Jeff and went out of the room.

It was light when Jeff woke up again. He knew it was time to get up this time. He carried his shoes to his mother's room. She always tied his laces and helped him button his shirt.

Mother wasn't in her room.

Jeff ran to the kitchen. Grandmother was always there to give him his cereal and juice.

Grandmother wasn't in the kitchen.

Jeff's big sisters, Rebecca and Andrea, were eating their breakfast.

"Where's Grandmother?" Jeff asked.

"Grandmother is sick." Rebecca buttered a slice of

toast for Jeff and poured milk into his cup.

"Where's Mother?" Jeff asked.

"Mother had to take Grandmother to the hospital," Rebecca answered. She buttoned Jeff's shirt, helped him put on his shoes, and tied his laces.

"They went in an ambulance," Andrea said.

"When will they come back?" Jeff asked.

Andrea began to cry. "Maybe Grandmother won't ever come home." Rebecca looked as though she wanted to cry too. Jeff wished Andrea would stop crying. He wished Mother and Grandmother were home with them right now.

Jeff ran out of the kitchen. He didn't feel hungry anymore. He went out to sit on the front steps to wait for his mother and his grandmother to come home.

Mr. Parker, the mailman, walked up the front steps to leave the mail. Jeff told him about Mother and Grandmother going away in an ambulance while he was asleep. "I'm waiting for them to come home, now," he said. Mr. Parker sat down with Jeff and visited for a little while; then he went away to leave mail at the other houses on the street.

Jeff waited. He waited for a long time. At last a taxi drove up and stopped. Jeff ran to meet his mother. She gave the taxi driver some money and got out of the taxi. Jeff was very happy to see her.

Rebecca and Andrea ran out to meet Mother. Jeff held onto his mother's hand so that they couldn't push him out of the way. They all walked into the house.

Mother told them that Grandmother was still very sick.

"Andrea says Grandmother won't ever come home," Jeff said.

Mother picked Jeff up and set him on her lap.

"I don't know whether she will or not," Mother said. "We have to wait and see."

"Does anybody know?"

"No."

Jeff wriggled down from his mother's lap. He didn't understand what was happening to his grandmother. He wished she were home right now.

20

7. Family Supper

"ISN'T it funny to be going to church at night!" Michael said to his father.

They were driving through quiet, almost dark streets to the church. They were going to a family supper. Michael's mother and his big sister Peggy were already there helping to get everything ready.

A light was on over the front door of the church. Some big boys and girls were sitting on the steps. They moved over to let Michael and his father get by.

"Hello, Mr. O'Connell," one of the boys said.

"Did you hear that?" Michael asked when they were inside. "He knew our name. Does everybody in the church know us now?"

"Quite a few do," Father answered. "After tonight we will know more people than we did, too."

They walked into the big room where they were going to eat supper. Mothers and fathers, grandmothers and grandfathers, and big and little children were standing around talking. Michael ran to the kitchen to find his mother.

"Look out!" someone shouted as Michael almost bumped into a lady carrying a hot dish. "Oh, hello, Michael," the lady said. His mother hurried over to him and gently pushed him out of the kitchen.

"I want you to stay out of the kitchen," she said. "Where are your father and Peggy?" she asked, then went back to the kitchen before Michael could tell her where they were.

Peggy was talking with some of her friends. Father was out in the hall talking with some other fathers. Michael looked around for someone to play with and saw Anne coming into the room with her mother and father and two older brothers. Anne was in his church school class.

Michael ran to meet her.

"My mother made a giant dish of spaghetti and meatballs," Anne said. She spread her hands to show how big.

"We can't go in the kitchen," Michael said.

"I know," Anne answered. "My father said I have to stay out of the way so he won't have to get spaghetti out of my hair again."

Anne and Michael walked around the room and looked at all the decorations their mothers had put on the tables.

"I know where the man puts his feet when he plays the organ," Anne said when they had finished looking at the tables.

Michael liked Anne most of the time. She usually had good ideas. They ran to the big room where the grown-ups went to church. It was dark.

"Do you know where to turn on the lights?" Michael whispered. Being in the dark always made him feel like whispering.

"Hello, what are you doing?" a voice said. Then the lights went on, and Michael saw Mr. Jones. Mr. Jones was one of his father's new friends.

"I know who you are," Anne said. "You are Ricky's father. And you are the minister, too."

"I know who you are," Mr. Jones answered. "You are Anne. And you"—he looked at Michael—"are Michael."

"We came to see where the man who plays the organ puts his feet." Michael explained.

"Well, let's go and look then," Mr. Jones said.

Michael had never been up on the platform where the organ was before. Part of the organ looked like a piano. On the floor were rows of thin boards.

"Those are the foot pedals." Mr. Jones said. "Mr. Randall presses those with his feet when he wants to play the low notes."

While Mr. Jones was telling Michael what all the knobs were for, Anne ran over to the big box that stood at the front of the platform.

"This is what you stand behind when you talk," she said. She tried to look over the top, but was too short, even on tiptoe.

"Yes," Mr. Jones answered. "It's called a pulpit."

"Will I ever talk from here?" Anne asked.

"Some day you may. When you are older, and when you have something that is important to you that you want to say to other people," Mr. Jones said.

"I have important things to say right now."

"I think you will have to wait until you can see over the top." Mr. Jones looked at his watch. "Let's go and see if supper is ready," he said.

Michael wished Anne didn't always talk so much. He wanted to find out more about the organ, but he followed Anne and Mr. Jones to the dining room.

Some people were sitting at the tables. Others were standing in a long line by the table nearest the kitchen. They were filling their plates with food. The whole

24

room smelled like food, and Michael felt hungry. He ran up to his parents who were standing in the line, and they helped him fill his plate. Then they went and sat down at one of the tables. Peggy was eating at another table with her friends.

Michael couldn't finish all the food on his plate. Some of it tasted good. Some of it tasted funny. None of it really tasted like the food his mother cooked at home. When he had eaten all he could, he sat back in his chair and listened to the grown-ups talking. Soon he was tired of sitting, and when he heard music he got up to see where it came from.

A big boy was playing a guitar in the next room. Big, little, and middle-sized children were sitting on the floor around him. Some were singing; others were just listening.

25

Mothers and fathers began to come into the room. Some of them sat on the floor and sang. Others went home with their children. Michael's parents stayed, and Michael crawled over to sit next to them.

Michael yawned and leaned against his father's arm.

"I think you are ready to go home to bed," Father said.

"No, I'm not!" Michael sat up straight. "I was yawning because I was comfortable." He was glad when he saw that his parents didn't really want to go home either. He yawned again. This time he climbed onto his father's lap and closed his eyes. Soon he was too sleepy to think about how much fun he was having. He would do that in the morning when he woke up.

8. First Snow

ALAN opened his eyes. It felt like morning, but the sun wasn't shining through his window shades. Maybe it was still night.

But it felt like morning.

Someone opened Alan's door. It was morning! Alan sat up in his bed.

"Hi, Alan," someone whispered. It was his big sister Althea. She tiptoed across the room and pulled up the window shade.

"Come and see what is happening."

Alan jumped out of bed and ran to the window.

"Snow!" he shouted. "It's snowing!"

"Sh!" Althea whispered. "Daddy and Mummy are still asleep."

Alan stood next to his sister and watched the snow fall. There were big and little flakes. The tops of the branches of the big cherry tree outside the window were white. Down on the ground there was no drive-

way, there was no lawn. It was all smooth and white.

A door across the hall opened.

"Now we can make a noise," Althea said.

"It's snowing, Daddy!" Alan shouted. "Come and see all the snow, Mummy."

Mother and Father came to the window. They didn't seem very excited. They didn't even look very happy, but they stood and looked out with Althea and Alan.

"It will take all morning to get that driveway shoveled," Father grumbled.

"I wish I had bought the groceries yesterday," Mother complained. "It's pretty, though," she said.

"Can I eat it?" Alan asked.

"Can we have pancakes for breakfast?" Althea wondered.

28

Father went to the bathroom to shave. Mother got dressed and went down to the kitchen to make breakfast. Althea and Alan hurried into their clothes.

After breakfast Alan went down to the basement with his father to help him look for the snow shovels. Althea went up to the attic with her mother to find their boots.

Then everybody went out into the snow. Flakes slid off Alan's cheeks and forehead, and settled on his nose and eyebrows. He put his head back, opened his mouth, and stuck out his tongue. A big flake landed there.

"It tastes good," he said.

"Snow doesn't taste," Althea said. She scooped up

29

a handful and lapped it with her tongue. Alan picked up some snow and tried it too as he started to walk down the driveway. The snow almost covered his boots.

"Look, Alan!" Althea shouted. "You made the first prints."

Alan looked behind him. He could see the deep marks in the snow that his boots had made.

Soon the driveway was full of boot prints. Father began to shovel the driveway. Mother shoveled the front walk. Althea and Alan started to help, but when they heard the snow plough coming down the street, they ran to watch it. It left piles of snow on both sides of the street.

"I hope it snows all day," Althea said.

"I hope it snows all day and all night and all tomorrow," Alan said.

Father grunted as he lifted another shovelful of snow.

Mother went inside because she said she could feel her nose turning purple.

9. A House for James

JAMES lived in an apartment house in the middle of the city. It was very tall and very old.

Father said their apartment was too small. Mother said it was too dark. James thought it was just right. His best friend, David, lived in the apartment just above his.

One day Father said, "I got the new job. Now we can buy a house."

"Where shall we look?" Mother asked.

"Why do we have to buy a house?" James asked.

"We need more room," Father answered. "We want you to have a yard to play in."

"Some day you will have brothers and sisters. We can't fit more people into two small rooms," Mother said.

31

"I have a sidewalk to play on and David to play with."

Later, when James went out to play, the sidewalk in front of the apartment house seemed wide and long, even though it was crowded with grown-ups and children and baby carriages.

Mr. Robbins, the building superintendent, was sitting on the steps in front of the apartment. He always sat there when he didn't have anything else to do. James sat down next to him.

"What's new?" Mr. Robbins asked.

"We need a house," James said.

"Houses are nice," Mr. Robbins said. "I lived in one once when I was a little boy."

"I like it here."

"If you find the right kind of house you will like that too."

They sat without talking for a while, watching the cars and trucks pass by on the street. Then James saw David pedaling up the sidewalk on his tricycle. He ran down the steps.

"Red light!" he shouted. David stopped and climbed off his tricycle. Just then they heard a siren. A fire engine clanged past. Then the hook and ladder roared by.

"Let's see where they are going," James said. They ran to the corner, but by the time they reached it, the hook and ladder was out of sight. They watched two taxi drivers arguing in the middle of the street. The cars behind them tooted their horns until a policeman came to tell the taxi drivers to move on.

It was growing dark. James and David ran back to the apartment building. James ran up two flights of stairs to his apartment. David ran up three flights to his.

While they were eating supper, James started to tell his mother and father about the taxi drivers.

"Your father and I have been thinking about the house," Mother said when he had finished his story.

James had forgotten all about that.

"Tomorrow we are going to look for a house," Father said.

"The right kind of house for us?" James asked.

33

10. The Right Kind of House

THE next morning James got into the car with his mother and his father. They drove through the city. Soon they left the tallest buildings behind them. They drove through streets where the apartments stood next to each other instead of on top of each other. They drove through streets where there were houses instead of apartments. They were very small and close together.

Father stopped the car in front of a small office building. The man behind the desk stood up when they walked inside.

"Mr. Walsh is going to help us find a house," Father said to James.

They got into their car again and followed Mr. Walsh's car through more streets. They passed a street where the houses were large and far apart.

"Will our house look like that?" James pointed to a big stone house. The front yard looked like a park he had seen once in the city.

"No, that would be too expensive for us."

"It's too big, anyway," Mother said.

James liked the big tree that grew in front of the house.

They drove through a street where the houses were smaller. They were very close together, and they all looked alike. "How will we know which is the right house?" James asked.

"When we see it, we will know."

Soon they stopped to look at houses. They looked at a red brick house, a gray house, a white house, two brown houses, and a yellow house. James looked at closets and cupboards with his mother. He looked at garages, attics, and furnaces with his father. Not one of the houses was the right kind of house.

"I'm hungry!" James said when they had finished looking at the yellow house.

"So am I," Father said. They stopped at a diner for lunch.

"I have one more place to show you," Mr. Walsh said after lunch.

James didn't feel like looking at any more houses. He wanted to go home, but he looked through the gray

35

stone house that Mr. Walsh wanted them to see. It wasn't the right house for them either. They said good-bye to Mr. Walsh and started back toward the city.

"Back to the apartment," Mother said. She didn't sound happy.

"Are you going to cry?" James asked.

"No," Mother answered, "but I am disappointed."

"Cheer up," Father said. "We'll look again another day."

"Why don't we just go on living at home?" James asked.

36

Suddenly Father stopped the car. "There's a 'For Sale' sign in front of that house," he said.

Mother looked at the house. "It's a little small," she said. "It needs painting." She looked a little longer. "I like what I see, though. Let's look inside." She opened the car door.

James looked at the house. It wasn't like any of the other houses on the street. They were new. They were all alike. This one was old and crowded between two new houses, but growing right beside it was a tree with low branches, and the sidewalk in front was wide. He climbed out of the car and followed his mother and father up the walk.

An old lady showed them through the house. She let Mother look in all her closets. She let Father go down to the basement to look at the wiring and the furnace. She told them that she was getting too old to take care of the house anymore. She wanted to live in an apartment.

James saw his mother and father look at each other. He saw them smile.

"Is this the right kind of house for us?" he asked.

"I think it is," Father answered.

11. Moving Out

JAMES sat on a trunk and looked out of the window. He held his stuffed elephant Ellie up so that she could look out too. "Tomorrow you won't see this street," he said. He looked at the tall buildings across the street. He looked down at the busy sidewalk. "Tomorrow we won't be here."

"Shall I pack Ellie with the rest of your toys, or would you like to keep her out?" Mother asked.

Most of his toys were already in a big brown box. "I'll keep her out," he decided. He started to poke through the box of toys.

"Please leave everything alone," Mother said. "You may unpack your box when we get to the new house."

"But I wanted to make sure you didn't forget anything."

"Why don't you go out and watch for the moving van?" Mother said.

Mr. Robbins was sitting in his usual place on the

front steps. "What's new?" he asked.

"I have to watch for the moving van," James said. He sat down. "Did you know I was moving today?"

"So this is the day you are leaving us." Mr. Robbins looked sorry. "We'll all miss you."

"I'll come back and visit you," James promised.

A big moving van drove up. It stopped in front of the apartment building, and two big men climbed out.

James jumped up. "I'll show you where to go." He ran ahead of the men to his apartment. "Mummy, they're here!" he shouted.

James ran up the next flight of stairs to David's apartment and banged on the door. "Hey, David," he shouted. "Come out and watch me move."

David's eyes grew wide when he saw the moving van. "Are you going to ride in that?" he asked.

"Of course not," James answered. "That's for our furniture." They squatted down on the sidewalk to watch. A crowd of people began to gather around. They all watched the movers carry furniture down the steps and into the moving van. James hoped everyone knew that it was his furniture and his van. "Be careful with that table!" he called out to the movers.

"I wish we could move," David said. "What's that under your arm?" He tugged at Ellie's ear.

James had forgotten all about her. "This?" He held her out by the tail. "This is a stinky old baby elephant." David grabbed Ellie and started to run. "Give it back," James shouted.

39

"You have to catch me first." David laughed.

James caught David easily. They wrestled for the elephant. An ear was missing when James finally got her back.

"James! You're getting your clothes all dirty." It was his father coming home from work.

James propped Ellie against the apartment building while he brushed off his pants. "Are we going now?" he asked.

"Let's go up and see if your mother is ready," Father said. James ran ahead. He stopped suddenly at the door of the apartment.

"It's all bare!" he said.

"Of course it is," Mother said. "The movers have taken everything."

James followed her around while she looked in empty closets and cupboards to make sure nothing was left behind. He began to feel a little strange. He didn't like the apartment this way. He ran down to the car.

"Good-bye, James," Mr. Robbins called from the front steps.

"Good-bye," David shouted.

James waved to everyone from the car window. "I think everyone is going to miss us," he said, as the car turned the corner.

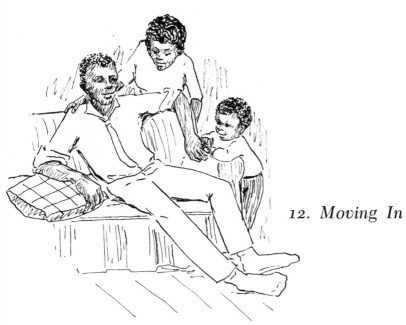

12. Moving In

THE new house was just as James remembered it. The wide sidewalk in front of the house and the tree in the side yard were still there.

The moving van was parked in front of the house.

"We're here," James called to the movers. "Are you going to move everything in now?" He stood and watched as the men began to carry all the furniture and boxes from the van into the house.

Some children from other houses watched the movers. They were watching James too. He began to feel strange.

Soon everything was moved in. The movers drove away. James ran inside.

"Whew, what a mess!" Father said. He sat down on the couch. There were boxes all over the living room. James's toy box wasn't there.

Mother walked into the living room. "I wonder what happened to that box of groceries," she said. She looked at Father. "Could you please set up James's bed while I get supper ready?"

Father groaned. Mother went back to the kitchen.

"Are you and Mummy cross with each other?" James asked.

"Not really," Father answered. "Your mother is tired, and I'm tired, and I bet you are too." He stood up. "Let's get that bed put together."

"I'm not tired." James ran up the stairs ahead of his father. He found his toy box in the middle of his room. He began to poke around in it.

"Hold this, please." Father held out the footboard to James.

James didn't move. He let out a yell.

Father dropped the footboard. "What on earth is the matter with you?" he asked.

"Ellie!" James howled.

Mother ran up the stairs. "What's the matter?"

"Ellie isn't here."

"Where is she?" Father asked.

"On the sidewalk at home." James started to cry.

"Are you sure?"

"I want Ellie," James said. "I want to go back to our apartment."

"I'll tell you what," Father suggested. "I'll stop by at the apartment house tomorrow morning on my way to work. Maybe Mr. Robbins found Ellie and is keeping her for you."

James stopped crying. He and his father finished

putting the bed together.

After supper Mother helped James unpack his toy box. He put his toys on the shelves in one corner of his room. He was so tired when he had finished that he let his mother undress him and get him ready for bed.

"I wonder were Ellie is right now," James said when his mother tucked his covers in.

"Would you like to take something else to bed with you tonight?" she asked. "What about your panda bear?"

James shook his head. "Tell me a story about Ellie."

Mother sat on the bed. She told him about the time he had left Ellie at the laundromat, how they had walked back and found her right where he had left her.

"She was on top of a washing machine," James said sleepily. Mother kissed him good-night and switched off the light.

James's new room looked very big in the dark. He was glad his mother had left the hall light on. He snuggled under the covers. His bed felt the same as it had in the apartment. The covers had the same smell. He reached out for Ellie. Then he remembered she wasn't there.

13. *A New Neighborhood*

JAMES opened his eyes. The sun shining through the window made him blink. He jumped out of bed.

"Mummy, where are you?" he called.

His mother's voice when she answered seemed very far away. James was used to hearing his mother moving around in the kitchen while he was still in bed. This morning, in his new house, he was all alone upstairs.

James ran downstairs to the kitchen. His mother was sitting at the table. He climbed onto her lap.

"Before I really woke up," he said, "I thought I was in our other home. But I didn't hear anything. Wasn't that funny? I didn't hear any trucks or any people, and I thought everyone had gone away."

"I think I'm going to have to get used to the quiet too," Mother said. She held James tight, then reached for the cereal and poured some into a bowl for him.

James slid off his mother's lap and sat beside her at the table. "Has Daddy gone to look for Ellie?" he asked.

44

"That's the first thing he is going to do when he gets into the city."

"I hope he finds her, don't you?"

"Yes."

After breakfast Mother helped James get dressed; then he went out to play.

First he went to the backyard. There were only flowers and grass there. He walked around to the side of the house to look at the tree growing there. The branches looked higher from the ground than they had yesterday. He climbed up onto the first branch. It was hard, but not too hard. He decided not to try the second branch and climbed carefully down from the tree to the ground. He walked to the front of the house.

The sidewalk still looked wide, but it was empty. The sidewalk in front of all the other houses on the street was empty too. James wondered who David was playing with this morning. There were always children to play with in front of the apartment building.

It was very quiet here. James didn't like its being so quiet. He ran inside to see what his mother was doing.

45

"We have to go to the store to buy a few things for the house and groceries for the weekend," Mother said when she saw James.

He followed her out of the front door.

"Where are the stores?" James asked. They had walked two blocks, and all he had seen were houses and grass.

"We have to walk to the end of the street," Mother answered.

"I hope we won't get lost." James held his mother's hand.

Mother stopped at the next corner and pointed to the street sign. "See that sign?" she said. "That tells us we are on 204th Street. That's our street. All we have to do is keep on this street until we come to the avenue where the stores are."

"Are we still on our street?" James asked after they had walked two more blocks.

"Yes, and we only have one more block to go."

They came to a wide street with stores on both sides and cars and buses roaring past both ways in the middle. The sidewalk was crowded with grown-ups, children, and baby carriages. It was very noisy. There were lots of things to look at.

James skipped happily beside his mother. "I think Daddy will find Ellie, don't you?"

"I certainly hope he does." Mother stopped at a hardware store. They went inside and bought a soap dish, some curtain rods, and a shopping cart.

James pushed the shopping cart to the supermarket. His mother had to push it out again because she had filled it with so many heavy bags of groceries.

They walked along the avenue back toward 204th Street. It was almost like being back on the street in front of the apartment. It was almost like it, but not quite. Mother didn't stop to talk to any of the people on the sidewalk. Nobody talked to James or his mother.

"Doesn't anybody here know us?" James asked.

"Not yet," Mother answered. "When we have lived here for a while, we will get to know some people."

They turned up their street and walked away from the noisy crowded avenue.

This time children were playing in front of their houses. Children were playing on the sidewalk in front of the house next door to James's own house. They looked at James. James looked at them. Then he ran to catch up with his mother.

47

14. *New Friends*

JAMES grew tired of watching his mother unpack boxes. He went outside to the backyard and looked at the grass. He wondered why there was so much grass around. It wasn't good for riding tricycles or bouncing balls.

He ran to the tree. He found that it was easier climbing onto the second branch than it had been when he tried it in the morning. He climbed higher into the tree. He climbed so high he could see into the yard next door.

The two children James had seen on his way home from the stores were playing on the grass in their backyard. They were turning somersaults and rolling around; they were having fun.

James shook the branch he was holding on to. The children stopped playing. James shook the branch again. The children walked over to the fence between James's yard and theirs.

"What are you doing?" the boy asked.

"Do you live here now?" the girl asked.

James climbed down from the tree. He forgot to be careful and fell from the last branch. The ground under the tree was soft. James sat still. He wasn't sure yet whether the fall from the tree hurt or not.

The boy and the girl crawled through the fence.
"What's your name?" the boy asked.
"James. What's yours?" James stood up.
"Peter. I'm four."
"I'm four too," James said.
"I'm Beth," the girl said.
"Beth is still a baby," Peter said. "She's only three."
"I'm not a baby!" Beth screamed. She jumped on Peter. James watched Beth and Peter roll around on the

49

ground as they had in their yard. He rolled beside them. Beth began to cry because Peter had pulled her hair.

"I can turn a somersault," Peter said after Beth had left. He put his hands on the ground, tucked his head under, and rolled over like a ball.

James tried to do the same thing, but he didn't roll over like a little ball. He fell sideways. He tried it again. Peter showed him how to tuck his head under, and this time he rolled over as Peter had.

James and Peter tried to do other tricks on the grass. When they were tired, they lay down on the soft grass. James looked up at the branches of the tree and at the sky. It was quiet and comfortable there. James liked his new yard. He liked his new friend.

"Peter!" a voice called from the yard next door.

Peter scrambled to his feet. "That's my mother," he said. "I think she's cross."

"Why is she cross?" James asked.

"Because she doesn't like me to pull Beth's hair." Peter ran toward his yard. "I'll see you in the morning!" he shouted to James as he ran around the other side of the fence.

James saw a light go on in his house. It must be almost time for supper. A car turned into their driveway. James ran to meet his father.

"Did you find Ellie?" James looked at the briefcase his father was carrying. That was all he was carrying.

"Here," his father said. He handed his briefcase to James. "Open it up."

50

James opened the bag. He put his hand in and felt something soft. He pulled out a stuffed elephant. It was squashed and very dirty, but it was Ellie. James tucked it under his arm. It just fit.

Suddenly James remembered all the things he wanted to tell his father.

"We went to the stores and didn't get lost," he said while his father kissed his mother. "I have two new friends, and Peter is going to be my best friend," he said while Father washed his hands. "My room is going to have new curtains, and we got a green soap dish for the bathroom," he said as they sat down at the table for supper.

15. Won't You Miss Me?

"I CAN'T play with you right now," James shouted to Peter from his bedroom window. "I'm packing." He turned back to his room and watched his mother pack neat piles of clean clothes into his suitcase.

"Now you can do the rest," Mother said.

James ran over to the shelves and came back to the bed with his arms filled with books and toy cars. He dumped them on top of his clothes, then put the cover down and latched it.

"Can I take my suitcase over right now?" he asked. He was very excited. He was going to stay next door with his best friend, Peter, for a whole week. He had never slept away from home alone before.

"Wait until Daddy comes home," Mother said. "He'll carry it over for you."

"Let me see how heavy it is." James grabbed the handle of the suitcase and dragged it off the bed. He carried it to the door and then let it drop. "The books make it heavy. I'll let Daddy carry it the rest of the way."

"Now let's pack your suitcase," James said. His mother was going to be at the hospital having a baby at the same time that James was going to be next door.

"It's all packed," his mother said. "Let's go downstairs now. Your father should be here any minute."

"Are you sure the baby will get born today?" James asked when they were settled on the living room couch.

"Yes," Mother answered.

"Was I born in the hospital too?" James asked.

"Yes. It was a different one."

"What was it like?"

"I told you yesterday, remember?"

"I want to hear about it today."

James listened while his mother told him about the hospital where he had been born.

"Won't you miss me?" he asked when she had finished.

"Yes, I will, but I won't be away very long."

"I know. It will be for just as long as I will be at Peter's house," James said. They had talked about that before too. Soon they heard a car door slam.

"We have been waiting for you for hours," James said when his father came in. He pulled at his sleeve. "Let's go upstairs and get my suitcase so I can start staying at Peter's house right now."

He ran up the stairs ahead of his father. He dragged his suitcase out into the hall. "It's very heavy," he warned. "It's the books and cars."

53

Mother was waiting for them at the foot of the stairs. She held out a sweater. "We forgot to pack this," she said. She leaned over to kiss James good-bye, then gave him a big hug.

"I think I'll miss you too," he said; then he wriggled out of her arms and ran down the steps to catch up with his father.

Peter's whole family met James and his father at the door. Peter's big brother took the suitcase upstairs. Peter and his little sister Beth danced around him. James began to feel important, and a little shy.

"Well, good night," he heard his father say. "I'll come over and see you tomorrow afternoon." He watched the front door close behind his father.

"Come and see your bed," Beth shouted. She took James's hand and tugged.

"He's my guest." Peter grabbed his other hand. "I'll show him."

54

"Why don't you both show him?" Peter's mother suggested.

James ran upstairs with Peter and Beth.

"That's your bed." Peter pointed to the bed next to his.

Later, when they were called to supper, James and Peter raced each other to the dining room. Then everyone sat down at the table and started to talk at the same time. Everyone but James was talking. He was thinking about his mother and father. He wondered where they were eating their supper. He took one bite of his hamburger and left the rest. He wasn't very hungry.

Later, when James and Peter went up to their room to go to bed, James took his books and cars out of his suitcase and put them at the foot of his bed. He saw Peter putting his pajamas on, so he took his out and put them on too.

"Where did your mother go?" James asked. At home his mother read him a story when he was ready for bed.

"I don't know. She's probably putting Beth to bed," Peter said. He sat on James's bed and picked up one of his cars.

55

They played with the cars until Peter's mother came in to say good night.

"Hop into your beds now," she said. She started to move James's cars and books over to the shelves at the other end of the room.

James sat up quickly. "My mother lets me keep my things on my bed," he said. He hoped he wasn't going to cry.

"I thought you would be more comfortable with them off your feet." Peter's mother smiled and put the books and cars back on James's bed.

"Your father called just before I came upstairs," she said while she tucked the covers in around James. She leaned over and said something that only he could hear, then went over to Peter's bed and tucked his covers in.

"What did my mother say?" Peter asked when his mother had gone downstairs.

"She said I have a baby brother," James answered.

"Oh." Peter yawned.

"She said he was born one hour ago. Do you know what a baby that's an hour old looks like?"

Peter didn't answer. He was asleep.

James tried to close his eyes, but they opened right up again. He wondered whether his new brother had stayed at the hospital with his mother or had come home with his father. He wondered if his mother was still missing him.

56

16. Too Old for a Baby-sitter

ERIC sat on the edge of the bathtub and watched his father shave.

"Why can't I go with you?" he asked for the fourth time since supper. He could see his father frowning at himself in the mirror.

"Because," his father answered, "this is not a party for four-year-olds."

"Why can't I just go with you and not go to the party?" Eric asked.

His mother stopped in the doorway. She was wearing curlers. "It's time for you to brush your teeth and get into your pajamas, dear," she said when she saw Eric. "I want you to be all ready for bed when the baby-sitter comes."

"I don't know where my pajamas are," Eric said, but his mother had hurried away. She didn't hear him.

"You can think about where they are while you brush your teeth," Father said. He handed Eric the big

tube of toothpaste. Eric squeezed some out without let-
ting any of the paste ooze into the washbasin, then
put the cap on. He brushed his teeth while his father
finished shaving.

Eric followed his father into the big bedroom. "I'm
too old to have a baby-sitter," he said. "Why do I have
to have one?"

"You are still too young to be left all alone in the
house at night," his father answered. "Now go and get
undressed."

"Then—" Eric had just thought of something. "Then
if I'm too young to leave alone, I'm too young to put
on my own pajamas."

Mother hurried into the bedroom. She had her best
dress on, but the curlers were still in her hair. "Please
go and get ready for bed, Eric," she said as she walked
past him. "Oh dear, I forgot to write down the telephone
number for Cathy."

"Why does Cathy need your number?" Eric asked.

"Just in case she should want to call us." Mother
left the room and hurried down the stairs again.

"Why would Cathy want to call you?" Eric asked
his father.

"You had better go and start looking for those pajamas," Father said. His voice was beginning to sound
cross.

Eric ran quickly to his room. He found his pajamas
on the chair. He got undressed and pulled on his pajama
bottom. Suddenly he remembered something. He ran out

58

to the hall and leaned over the banister. "My story, Mummy," he shouted. "You forgot to read me my story."

"Cathy will do that when she comes," his mother answered. She was on her way up the stairs, and she walked past Eric into the bedroom.

"I don't want Cathy to read to me," Eric said. "I don't want Cathy to baby-sit. I don't want anyone to baby-sit." He walked to his parents' room and sat down on the floor. "I want you to stay home tonight." He put his thumb in his mouth. He saw both parents look at him, then turn around to finish what they were doing. He watched his mother brush her hair. He watched his father polish his shoes. He took his thumb out of his mouth. It didn't taste or feel as good as it had when he was two, or even three.

"I can remember when I was a brand-new baby," Eric said suddenly and loudly. His mother and father turned and looked at him again. "I remember you stayed home all the time, but if you had to go to a party, you always took me with you. You never left me with a baby-sitter." His mother and father were all dressed. They looked different.

"Is that right?" Father asked.

"That's funny," Mother said. "I remember the first time we left you with a baby-sitter."

"You do?" Eric asked. "When was that?"

"It was when you were a baby. You were almost six months old," Mother said. She smiled. "Your father and I came home and found you and the baby-sitter

59

on the couch. You were both crying."

"Why was I crying?" Eric asked.

"Your gums were sore. The next day your first tooth appeared."

"Oh, yes, I remember," Eric said. "I forget, was the baby-sitter getting teeth too?"

"No, I think she was a little frightened by your howling," Father said. "You had the loudest howl of any baby in the neighborhood."

Eric laughed. "I don't howl anymore," he said. He pulled his pajama top over his head. "I was stupid then. I couldn't even put on my own clothes."

"Of course you couldn't. You were a baby," Mother said. She hugged Eric. The doorbell rang, and Eric wiggled out of her arms.

"I'll get it," he said. He rushed down the stairs and opened the front door.

"Hi, Cathy," Eric said. "You know what?"

"What?" Cathy asked.

"You aren't my baby-sitter anymore. You know why?"

"Why?"

"Because I'm not a baby anymore. That's why," Eric said.

17. The House on the Hill

"I SAW the mountain first!" Linda shouted. "We're almost there!"

"That isn't a mountain. It's a hill," Paul said. He leaned forward. "It's a hill, isn't it, Dad?"

"It's a very steep hill," their father answered. He shifted the car into low and started it up the hill.

When they came to a curve in the road, Linda shut her eyes. She opened them again, and there was the big white house on top of the hill.

The car stopped, and Grandmother and Grandfather came out to greet them. Linda and Paul and their mother and father climbed out of the car.

"Paul and I are going to live with you," Linda said. She was so excited that she was hopping up and down.

"We are just visiting them, Linda," Paul corrected her.

"But while you are visiting we can say you are living with us, can't we?" Grandfather said. "Let's see how heavy you are now that you are four." He lifted Linda up to his shoulders and walked into the house.

Father came in with Paul's and Linda's suitcases. "Where shall I put these?" he asked.

"Let's see." Grandmother thought for a while.

"On the porch," Linda said. "We're sleeping on the porch, aren't we?"

"Why, yes," Grandmother said, "on the porch. That's a good place."

Linda laughed. "We always sleep there." She saw Paul following his father up the stairs, and she ran after them.

There were two cots on the sleeping porch. Linda knew which one was hers. The old doll that her mother had played with when she was a little girl was lying on the pillow. Linda picked it up and rocked it in her arms. "Aren't you glad to see me?" she sang. "I'm going to be here for two whole weeks."

"Come and say good-bye to Mom and Dad," Paul called to her.

Linda put the doll down quickly. She had almost forgotten about that. Her mother and father weren't going to stay at Grandmother and Grandfather's this time. They were going away to have a vacation by themselves. "Wait for me!" Linda screamed. She hoped they hadn't gone away without saying good-bye. She ran into the living room. They were still there.

"Don't go yet." Linda held on to her mother.

"I'm afraid we have to," Mother answered. "We want

62

to get there before dark."

"We have a long drive ahead of us," Father said.

Linda and Paul and their grandparents followed Mother and Father out to the car. They waved until the car disappeared around the curve. Linda could hear it going down the hill; then everything was quiet. Grandmother put her arm around Linda's shoulders.

"Your grandfather and Paul are going down to look at the pond," she said. "Do you want to go with them, or do you want to come inside with me?"

"I want to come with you," Linda answered. She skipped beside her grandmother into the kitchen. She watched her start a pie for their supper, then began to wonder what Paul was doing.

"I think I'll go to the pond," she said suddenly.

"All right." Grandmother put the pie in the oven. "Do you remember the way?"

"Yes." Linda ran outside. She found the path to the pond behind the shed. The tall grass at the sides of the path tickled her legs as she ran. Soon she could hear voices, and she saw Paul and Grandfather on the far side of the pond.

"Come here," Peter shouted when he saw her. "We found some tadpoles."

Linda watched her grandfather and Paul bending over the water. It looked as though they were having fun. Suddenly she wished that she had come to the pond with them. Now she would have to walk along the edge of the pond by herself. If she asked her grandfather to

63

come back for her, Paul would call her a baby. She wished her mother and father hadn't gone away and left her. Her mother would have understood her being afraid of things. She sat down on a patch of dry ground and sniffled.

"Linda, come here!" Paul shouted. "I caught two tadpoles. One is for you."

Linda couldn't remember what a tadpole looked like. She stood up and looked for a path that wasn't so close to the water. She found a place where the grass didn't grow too high, and she walked along that until she reached her grandfather and Paul.

Paul handed her a tin can. She looked down at the

64

little black things swimming around in the water and felt a little disappointed. "Oh, I remember those." She scooped one of the tadpoles out of the can and threw it into the pond.

"What did you do that for?" Paul asked.

"So it can be with its mother," Linda answered.

Paul dumped the rest of the water and the tadpole into the pond. "I can catch some more tomorrow," he said. "Let's go home."

It was just beginning to grow dark when they reached the house. They could smell supper cooking when they opened the door.

18. *First Day of School*

JAMES sat on the lowest branch of his climbing tree in the side yard. His mother had sent him outside to play because he was going to have to be inside all afternoon. He watched a yellow leaf fall from a branch above him. Soon all the leaves on this tree would be yellow. Then they would fall to the ground and leave the branches bare. James could remember how the tree looked almost a whole year ago. The branch he was sitting on began to shake.

"Hi! I scared you."

James turned around and saw Peter. Peter lived next door.

"I knew you were there," James said. "I could hear you sneaking over from your yard."

"No, you didn't. I surprised you." Peter climbed up and sat next to James. "Now you try to surprise me."

James climbed down and ran around to the other side of his house. He waited awhile, then walked slowly and very quietly across the lawn toward the tree again. Just before he reached the tree, he stepped on a pile of dry leaves.

"I heard you!" Peter turned around quickly before James could touch the tree. This was their newest game, to sneak up on each other without being heard.

James shook the branch. Peter jumped off, and they rolled around in the dust under the tree until they were tired and needed a rest.

"I wonder what school will be like," James said after they had rested for a while.

"I was thinking that too." Peter looked surprised. "How did you know I was thinking that?"

"Let's do it again," James suggested. They were quiet for a while.

"I'm thinking that I hope we can sit next to each other," James said.

"I was thinking that too." Peter said. "And I was thinking that the teacher will say, 'Don't you know how to tie your shoelaces yet? You naughty boy, go home!'"

"Then she'll say, 'You have to read a thousand books this afternoon or you can't go home!'"

They both giggled; then they made up some more funny things for the teacher to say. They didn't hear James's mother walk up behind them.

"I'm thinking that it's time for you to come in for lunch," she said to James.

"My mother said that as soon as lunch was finished it would be time to go to school." Peter stood up and ran to his house.

James gulped down his sandwich while his mother fed his baby brother. "I have to eat a lot now because I'll be too busy learning in school to eat."

His mother nodded. "If you're hungry after school, you may have a snack then."

"The trouble is—" James frowned. "The trouble is, I don't know what I am going to learn."

"Your teacher will let you know that," Mother said. "I think that today you will start to learn how to get used to being in school."

"That will be easy." James swallowed the last of his sandwich, then ran upstairs to change his clothes.

He was all dressed when his mother came in to see if he needed any help. She was holding the baby.

"Look." James lifted one foot. "I tied my shoelaces."

"Good," Mother said. "You look nice." She looked at the baby. "See how handsome your big brother looks, Donny."

68

"He knows what you are saying," James said. "He shook his head up and down." He tickled Donny under his fat chin. "When you are big like me, you will go to school too." The baby wiggled in his mother's arms and tried to grab James's nose.

Mother tucked a clean handkerchief into James's shirt pocket; then they went outside. Mother put Donny into his stroller. They met Peter and his mother and his little sister Beth in front of their house, and they all started to walk to the school together.

The school was three blocks away. James and Peter ran ahead of their mothers, the stroller, and Beth. When they saw the school, they began to walk more slowly to let their mothers catch up with them.

"You may come inside with me if you want to," James whispered to his mother when they reached the front door.

"I would like to," Mother whispered back. She lifted Donny from his stroller, and they followed Peter and his mother and Beth into the big sunny classroom.

Miss Miles, the teacher, was at the door to meet them. When James told her his name, she gave him a blue name tag to pin to his shirt. Then she showed him where to sit.

James sat down in his chair at a round table. The other children at the table were looking at books and playing with puzzles. He looked down at the puzzle in front of him. He liked putting puzzles together, but he didn't feel like doing it right away. He looked for Peter.

He saw him sitting at a table on the other side of the room. He wanted to get up and sit in the empty chair next to Peter but didn't feel like moving from his seat. He turned around and saw that his mother and Donny were leaving. He waved to them, then turned back to his puzzle and started to put the pieces together.

19. *Shopping*

MOTHER helped Timmy tie the hood of his snowsuit.

She buttoned her own jacket, picked up her gloves, her pocketbook, and her shopping list. This was the day for Timmy and his mother to go shopping.

They went to the library first. A lady showed Timmy a table where the new picture books were kept. She told him he could take any book he liked. Timmy found a book filled with pictures of cars and trains. The lady wrote something on a card. She said Timmy could keep the book for two weeks. Timmy looked at his book while his mother looked for a book for herself. She took a long time.

"Can we have some juice now?" Timmy asked when they left the library.

"Not yet." Mother looked at her list. "I have to buy some paint."

They walked into the hardware store next to the library. Timmy looked at all the tools and nails in one part of the store while his mother looked for a can of paint. She took a long time.

"Now can we have some juice?" Timmy asked when they left the hardware store.

"Not yet," Mother said. "I have to get stamps at the post office first."

They crossed the street and went into the post office. There were long lines of people in front of the windows. Timmy waited in line with his mother. There was nothing to look at. Everything was too high for Timmy to see anything. He and his mother had to wait for a long time.

"Now we can have some juice," Timmy said when they left the post office.

"Yes," Mother said.

They went into the five-and-ten-cent store where the counter was low, where Timmy could climb up onto the stool by himself. There were other people at the counter. Timmy didn't know any of them, but he knew the lady behind the counter. She knew Timmy, and she knew what kind of juice he wanted. She knew Timmy's mother wanted a cup of hot coffee. They had been there before.

Timmy drank all his juice with a straw. He waited for his mother to finish her coffee. She took a long time.

"I want to look at the toys," Timmy said when they left the counter.

Timmy knew where the toys were kept in this store. He ran ahead of his mother. He looked at the balls— big round bright balls, white plastic baseballs, and foot-

72

balls. He saw a football just like the one he had at home. He passed a row of dolls. There were more dolls there than his sister had in her room at home. He stopped in front of the cars. There were cars big enough to ride on. There were cars that ran with batteries. Timmy knew, because he had one of those at home. There were tiny cars that could fit into a pocket. Timmy picked up one of them, a tiny red racing car. It fit very nicely in his hand. He looked at it for a long time.

"Hurry up, Timmy," Mother said. "I have more shopping to do."

"I need a racing car," Timmy said.

"You have enough cars at home," Mother said. "Put it down now."

Timmy put the racing car back on the counter. He looked at it a little longer. He didn't have a tiny red racing car.

"Come on, Timmy!" Mother started to walk away from the counter.

Timmy picked up the racing car. He wanted to see what it felt like in his hand again. Mother was two counters away. Timmy didn't want to let the racing car out of his hand again. He closed his fingers over it. Now he couldn't see it, but he could still feel it.

Mother was almost at the door.

Timmy ran to catch up with his mother.